Meet the Mayor

Arnim Franke

REAL LIFE readers™

Rosen Classroom™
New York

A city is a large **community** that has many people, roads, and buildings.

Every city has a **government**.
The government makes laws.
Laws help keep people safe.

Many city governments have a leader
called a **mayor**.
People **vote** for the person they want
to be mayor.

The mayor promises to work hard

and be a good leader.

The mayor works at a building called

city hall.

Other government leaders work there, too.

The mayor helps make laws and rules.
What laws and rules do you know?
How do they help people?

A mayor does many things each day. Sometimes a mayor gives a **speech** about the city.

A mayor talks to people all over the city. They tell the mayor what they need and what they want.

The mayor works hard for the people.

The mayor makes the city a better place to live!

A Mayor's Day

arrives at city hall

meets with voters

discusses new laws with city workers

gives a speech

has a dinner meeting with park workers

goes home

Glossary

city hall The building where a city's leaders work.

community A place where people live and work together.

government The people who make laws.

mayor The leader of a city government.

speech A talk given to a group of people.

vote To choose someone or something.